Printed in the U.S.A.

ISBN 0-7172-8300-3

JIM HENSON'S MUPPETS IN

The Trouble with Twins

A Book About Jealousy

By Bonnie Worth • Illustrated by Tom Leigh

GROLIER

One crisp fall morning, a crowd of kids gathered to watch Skeeter perform tricks with her new, super-duper yo-yo.

"Wow," said Piggy. "Where did you get that?"

"From my uncle Skipper," said Skeeter. "He gave Scooter one, too. He always gives us the same present, because we're twins."

"Could you teach me how to use it?" asked Kermit.

"Sure," said Skeeter. "It's easy."

"Easy, my foot," muttered Scooter. He couldn't get the yo-yo to do anything. He tried to get it to go up and down, but it just hung from its string.

It was just like the time the twins had both gotten pogo sticks. Skeeter had learned to bounce on hers a hundred times without stopping. Scooter couldn't even get *up* onto his. And then there was the time they'd gotten juggling beanbags. Skeeter had learned to juggle three of them at once. Scooter couldn't even juggle *one*.

All that morning in school, Skeeter performed amazing yo-yo stunts while the other kids *ooh*ed and *aah*ed . . .

in the cafeteria . . .

at recess . . .

and in gym class, where even the teacher was impressed.

Watching Skeeter get all the attention made Scooter feel jealous. It was always the same story. Everything was so easy for her, and so hard for him. Nobody even noticed him. Why couldn't he be a star like Skeeter?

At the end of the day, Ms. Palmer, the science teacher, made an announcement.

"One month from today is the annual science fair, class. I want each one of you to prepare a project. The best project will win the grand prize."

Everyone was excited, especially Scooter.
Science was his favorite subject.

Hmmmm, he thought. *I wonder what I should do.*

When Scooter happened to look over at Skeeter, though, he saw she didn't look excited. She looked worried.

In fact, she was so worried that she dropped her yo-yo. It rolled across the floor.

"Skeeter, please put that away," said Ms. Palmer. "Science class is no place for yo-yos."

Later, at home, Skeeter came into Scooter's room.

"What are you doing for your project?" she asked him.

"I'm going to make a rocket," he said.

"Wow!" said Skeeter. "I don't know what to do. But I guess I'll think of something."

I'm sure she will think of something, thought Scooter. *She always does.*

By the end of the week, Skeeter had come up with an idea.

"What is it?" Scooter asked.

"I'm making a model of the solar system, using fruit," she told Scooter.

"That sounds very creative," he said.

Gonzo stood outside the window. "C'mon, Skeeter!" he called. "You were going to show me how to 'walk the dog'!"

"Bye, Scooter," said Skeeter, and she ran out.

And so, the next day, Skeeter got a grape-fruit for the sun, and oranges and lemons for the planets. She hung them by strings from a long stick and labeled them.

"Now I'm ready for the science fair," she said to Scooter, and she dashed off to teach Kermit and Piggy yo-yo tricks.

A week later, Scooter had to give Skeeter some bad news. "Don't look now," he said, "but your solar system is starting to rot. There are flies all over the sun."

"Oh, no!" Skeeter moaned, dragging it off to the garbage. "I can't even make another one. It has to be at the fair for a *week*!"

There were now only two more weeks till the science fair. Skeeter got some clay and began working it. She pounded and pulled and molded it for days before she showed it to Scooter.

"Well...what do you think of it?" she asked anxiously.

Scooter looked up from his rocket. "What *is* it?" he wanted to know. "A slug?"

Skeeter sagged. "No! It's supposed to be a scale model of a robin redbreast! Oh, why can't I be good at science like you?"

Only a week until the science fair!
Skeeter had one more idea. She would press
wildflowers and give their scientific names.
She went outside and picked some flowers,
and pressed them into the pages of a book.

"Whew!" she said. "I'm glad I took care of
that." And she ran off to perfect a new trick
with her yo-yo.

But the day before the science fair, when Skeeter went to take the flowers out of her book, she found they had crumbled and turned to dust. "Oh, no!" she wailed. "The science fair is tomorrow, and I still don't have a project!"

"I have an idea," said Scooter. "Why don't you do a yo-yo demonstration?"

"You heard Ms. Palmer," Skeeter told him. "Science is no place for yo-yos."

"It is if you use a yo-yo to explain the laws of motion and gravity," said Scooter.

"That's a great idea!" said Skeeter. "You're so smart! You're so practical! I've always wished I could be more like you."

"You have?" laughed Scooter. "But you're always the center of attention. I've always wished I could be like *you*!"

Skeeter started laughing too. They laughed so hard, they fell on the floor.

The next day, there was a big crowd at
the science fair. They watched Skeeter's
yo-yo demonstration. Then they moved on to
see Piggy's garbage garden, Kermit's rock
collection, and all the other projects.

And finally, they rushed outside to see Scooter launch his rocket. All eyes were on him. This time, Scooter was the center of attention!

He began the countdown. "5, 4, 3, 2, 1, blast off!" Into the sky went Scooter's rocket.

"Hurray!" everyone cheered.

"The grand prize for Most Spectacular Project goes to Scooter!" announced Ms. Palmer at the end of the fair.

"Good going, Scooter!" said everyone.

"And Skeeter wins a certificate for Most Practical Project," added Ms. Palmer.

"This certificate should really go to you," said Skeeter as they walked home. "I mean, it was your idea."

"I have a way you can pay me back," said Scooter. "You can teach me how to yo-yo."

"It's a deal!" said Skeeter, with a grin.

So they ran home together, holding their prizes—and glad to be exactly who they were.

Let's Talk About Jealousy

If you've ever felt jealous of someone else, you know that it isn't a good feeling. But it happens to everyone. You can be jealous of someone's things, or their talents, or the friends they have.

Scooter and Skeeter needed to remind each other of what made each of them special. Then they didn't feel jealous anymore.

Here are some questions about jealousy for you to think about:

Have you ever been jealous of someone? What were you jealous of? How did it make you feel?

Do you think anyone has ever been jealous of you?

When you're jealous, what can you do or say to yourself that would make you feel better?